KEENAN

On Call Back Mountain

ON CALL BACK

Eve Bunting

MOUNTAIN

Illustrated by Barry Moser

THE BLUE SKY PRESS

An Imprint of Scholastic Inc. • New York

OUR FARM is at the bottom of Call Back Mountain, on the very edge of the wilderness. And as soon as fire season begins, my brother and I start watching for Bosco Burak to come along the trail.

Way up on Call Back is a fire tower. Bosco has been lookout in that tower every summer since before forever. He's our friend. Each June, when he and his mules Aida and Traviata pack in, they spend the first night with us. The next morning, they climb the fifteen-mile trail to the tower.

"There he is!" I yell.

Bosco waves. "Howdy, Joe! Howdy, Ben!"

It's been so long since we've seen him that Ben and I are a bit shy. We pet the ladies, which is what Bosco calls his mules. Then Bosco tells us to stand against the larch tree so he can measure us.

"Two inches," he says, squinting at last year's marker.

Ben and I nudge each other and grin. We want to be tall, like Bosco. He has the longest, skinniest legs in the whole world. Cherry pickers, he calls them. Ben and I have been dangling ourselves from that larch tree to stretch our bones, and it has really paid off. Mom and Dad rush out to hug Bosco while we take care of the ladies. Then Ben and I carry in the big Morton salt box that holds Bosco's CDs and tapes.

He has brought new books for us and puzzles and games.

"We're going to have a 'specially good supper tonight 'cause you're here," Ben tells him.

"It's elk roast," I say. "And two kinds of vegetables."

While everything cooks, Ben and I read to Bosco so he can see how many new words we've learned in school.

Ben shows him how he has stopped
chewing his fingernails and teaches
him to play a new game.
"Give me a high, bye! Bye!
"Give me a low, too slow!"
We're not shy anymore.

"See any wolves yet?" Bosco asks Dad.

Dad hulls the last gooseberry for the gooseberry pie. "Not a one," he says.

Bosco smiles. "They'll be back. The coyotes are back. Any creature that loves the wilderness will always come back."

It was the fire a few summers ago that drove the wolves away, the wolves and coyotes and the other animals, too.

"The fire wasn't your fault, Bosco," Ben says. He said that last year. The year before last, too.

"Thanks, pal," Bosco tells him.

We know it wasn't Bosco's fault. That fire had been set in three places, and even his quick alarm couldn't save it. But now the forest is beginning to grow again. Bosco says it won't be too long till it's thick and healthy as ever.

Dad puts the gooseberry pie in the oven. "Haven't seen as much as a wolf track, Bosco," he says. "So far you're the only lone wolf up there."

Bosco throws his head back and howls a lone wolf howl. "Woooo!"

"That's the call for supper," Mom tells us.

I quickly get my bird book to show Bosco the birds I've seen and drawn this year. "Here's a pileated woodpecker. This is a great horned owl."

"Nice!" Bosco points to a drawing. "Did you know the great horned owl is called the tiger of the night?"

"Cool!" I say. And I think, *I have seen the tiger of the night.*

After supper we move onto the porch. Bosco puts a CD into the player.

Mr. Enrico Caruso sings for us.

He sings for us all through the long, white twilight. Later, when Ben and I are in bed, we can still hear him.

Pale moths swoop like ghosts against our window screen.

My fingers smell of gooseberry pie.

And Mr. Enrico Caruso, the greatest tenor the world has ever known, sings us to sleep.

Bosco leaves for his mountain early in the morning.

We watch till he and the ladies turn the bend in the trail, and I can tell Ben's trying not to cry.

"Don't blubber," I say. "He'll be back in two or three months." But I'm trying not to blubber myself. Summer lasts a long while.

All day long we wait for the dark to come down. As soon as it does, Mom and Dad light the two lanterns for Ben and me, and we all go down to the meadow where the woods begin.

Ben and I hold the lanterns high.

Way up on Call Back, a light answers ours.

"Good night, Bosco," we shout.

All through the summer we send our good nights across the darkness, and it's as if Bosco is still with us. Until, one night, no light answers ours.

"Where *is* he?" Ben asks.

Mom looks nervously at Dad.

Dad puts his hands on my shoulders. "Come morning, Mom and I'll hike up there and check things out."

"Can I come?" I ask.

Mom shakes her head. "I'd like it if you'd stay here with Ben."

They leave at first light.

Ben's chewing on his fingernails again. "What do you think happened?"

"Probably nothing," I say. But I don't feel very good about this. Bosco always answers our light.

Around noon we see a fire helicopter heading for the tower.

"Dad must have called the park service on Bosco's two-way radio," I tell Ben.

"But *why*?" Ben asks.

"I don't *know* why," I say. "How would *I* know why?"

In about an hour the copter whirs back. Ben and I keep running down to the meadow, watching for Mom and Dad.

When they come, they have Aida and Traviata with them.

"We knew the ladies wouldn't be able to get along on their own, so we brought them," Mom says. I can tell she's been crying.

"But where's Bosco?" Ben asks.

Mom smoothes his hair. "Bosco had a heart attack, Ben. He died up there, on his mountaintop."

I think I knew it before Mom said it. I think I knew from the way she and Dad looked.

"We sat beside him till the copter came," Dad says. "And Mr. Caruso sang for him."

My throat hurts. I run to Dad, and he puts his arms around me, and then Ben runs to Dad, too, and then Mom runs, and we cling together.

"Bosco!" Ben wails. "Bosco!"

I glance sideways at the ladies. They're standing so quietly, their heads hanging. Do they know? Poor ladies.

"Will they send someone to take his place?" I ask Dad.

"They told me they wouldn't. Not this year."

"Nobody *could* take his place," I say.

Dad's arms tighten around me. "No. Nobody could."

That night I wake up, and Ben's not beside me.

I know where he is.

The outside air is warm. The grass is crunchy under my bare feet. Down where the woods begin, I see a flash of light.

"Ben!" I yell.

He turns. "I keep telling Bosco good night. But he doesn't answer. I thought it was a mistake, him being dead."

I take the lantern. Ben's way too little to be carrying it out here
by himself. Mom and Dad would have a fit.

I can't think of anything to say to make him feel better because I
feel so awful myself.

A woodcock calls. I hear the cry of a tiger of the night.

Above us, on a ledge of darkness, a shadow moves, then
stands. It looks down on us with great, shining eyes.

"It's a wolf," I whisper. "A lone wolf."

Ben moves closer to me.

"You don't have to be scared," I tell him.

The wolf watches us, then steps back and disappears into
the darkness. That wolf had the longest, skinniest legs.

"Cherry pickers," I whisper.

"What?"

"Nothing." I take Ben's hand. "Remember what Bosco said?
Any creature that loves the wilderness will always come back?"

Ben nods. "I remember."

Somewhere in the near darkness a wolf howls. . . . "Woooo."
Ben's fingers hold tight to mine. "Bosco would be pleased about
the wolf," he whispers.

"Yes," I say. "Bosco would be pleased."

THE BLUE SKY PRESS

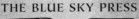

Text copyright © 1997 by Eve Bunting
Illustrations copyright © 1997 by Barry Moser

For information regarding permission, please write to:
Permissions Department,
The Blue Sky Press, an imprint of Scholastic Inc.,
555 Broadway, New York, New York 10012.

The Blue Sky Press is a registered trademark of Scholastic Inc.

Library of Congress Cataloging-in-Publication Data
Bunting, Eve, 1928-
On Call Back Mountain / Eve Bunting; illustrated by Barry Moser.
p.   cm.
Summary: Two brothers encounter a lone wolf on the spot
where each summer night before they had signaled their friend
the fire watchman up on the mountain tower.
ISBN 0-590-25929-6
[1. Friendship—Fiction.   2. Death—Fiction.   3. Wolves—Fiction.
4. Fire lookout stations—Fiction.]   I. Moser, Barry, ill.   II. Title.
PZ7.B915270m   1997   [E]—dc20 96-19983   CIP AC

12 11 10 9 8 7 6 5 4 3 2 1   7 8 9/9 0 1 2/0

Printed in the United States of America   37

The illustrations in this book were executed with watercolor on paper
handmade by Simon Green at the Barcham Green Mills in Maidstone,
Kent, Great Britain, especially for the Royal Watercolor Society.
Production supervision by Angela Biola
Art direction by Kathleen Westray
Designed by Barry Moser

First printing: May 10, 1997
in memory of Scott Fischer